Cigarettes
In the Rain

Cigarettes
In the Rain

An Anthology

By

A.B. Hughes

[Bad Liver Press]

www.ABHughes.com

Printed in the United States of America

ISBN-13: 978-0692375914
ISBN-10: 0692375910

Published by:
Bad Liver Press
P.O. Box 5344
Toms River, New Jersey
08754

www.BadLiverPress.com

To my irresistible urge to keep drinking.

Contents

(7:15 PM) At a Café around Dusk   11
7:15 PM   13
(7:30 PM) The Young Man at the Train Station   15
(8:00 PM) The Young Woman and the Papers   19
(9:00 PM) The Man and the Rain   20
(9:30 PM) The Girl and the Music   22
9:45 PM   23
(10:30 PM) In the Starlit Night   25
(11:00 PM) Going Home   28
(11:30 PM) The Drunk   31
(12:15 AM) The Old Woman and the Rain   36
12:45 AM   39
(1:00 AM) In Search of Something Warm   41
(1:30 AM) A Veteran at the Park   43
1:45 AM   45
(2:00 AM) Late Night Wine   47
(2:30 AM) For that Moment   49
2:45 AM   51
(3:00 AM) At a Rest Stop on the Freeway   53
(3:30 AM) Remembering Vera   56
3:45 AM   61
(4:15 AM) Probably Just another Moment   63
5:00 AM   65
(5:30 AM) Cigarettes and the Rain   67

"there is a loneliness in this world so great
that you can see it in the slow movements of
the hands of a clock"

-    Charles Bukowski, "The Crunch"

(7:00 PM) At a Café around Dusk

"Are you okay?"

"She left me, man."

"Yeah, I know."

He sat in the old chair that creaked when he moved and stared out the café window. The room was dim. It was a good place to drink coffee, and there were chess tables. I didn't think he was in the mood for a game. There were hipsters reciting poetry I never heard before. Most of them were quiet and nice, and the poetry wasn't too bad. Others were loud and it ruined the poetry.

"How can I help you?" The waitress had a pleasant smile. We ordered coffee.

"I can't believe this happened." He said, loosening his tie.

The waitress returned with the coffee. It tasted watered down to me, but he took a great gulp of it just the same.

"What am I supposed to do now, man?"

"Live, I suppose." I took a sip of the coffee.

"How am I supposed to do that?"

I didn't have an answer for him. I wasn't any good in those conversations. I just wanted him to keep waking up in the morning.

We stayed in the café for a few hours. I let him talk when he needed to. I also let him stay quiet when he needed to. He did a lot of both. I felt lousy for not being much help. I started the car, and we pulled out of the driveway.

"Can we stop there again?" He asked.

"Sure."

I lit a cigarette and offered him one. He smoked it and turned his eyes to the sky. It was about dusk, and the sky was very beautiful. When the car stopped, he put out his cigarette and walked off. I waited in the car and watched him shrink little by little in the distance. He sunk down by the tombstone, and I just thought, dear God, please, please don't let this ever happen to me.

7:15 PM

After dusk, the crystal lakes sparkle in a deep blue, and if the water is calm and still and the sky as clear as it should be, the water reflects the stars, and it's like looking into a mirror straight into the heart of heaven. The sailors know the beauty of the water, and the fish, and the birds that fly overhead. But the men and women, driving too fast in their passing automobiles, miss the beauty each time; concerned with other things, bills, soccer games, groceries – and in that moment, the bum sitting beside the bridge, dreaming over the shores of the deep crystal, becomes that much closer to knowing god and seeing him how he should be seen.

(7:30 PM) The Young Man at the Train Station

It was an unusually cold evening. It rained, leaving the air unpleasant. A young man sat at the train station and watched as the trains pulled away. He was there often. He would sit at the bench, smoke cigarettes, drink coffee, and watch until he couldn't bring himself to watch any longer. He liked to watch the trains. They reminded him of his childhood, when he would watch the soldiers return home. He remembered it so well. They had girlfriends, children, wives, or mothers waiting for them. Sometimes, they had no one to greet them. He remembered the look in their eyes, a pained look, when no one was there.

The young man must have looked dirty. He had that way about him. He stopped caring, but he forgot the reason. Sometimes, passengers would lay money down beside him. He'd just smile and thank them. He wasn't poor though, and he wasn't homeless. He just felt like he was. He had always felt that way.

He tried to run away once. He joined the Army a couple of winters back. He had high hopes, dreams even, but they all fell and broke apart one by one. There was a war, but he missed it. He missed out on the honor, the pride, the awards; he missed out on all of it. His head got in the way. There was

15

nothing that could have been done. It wasn't his fault. Somehow, he had to realize that, but he blamed himself anyway. When he returned home, he had no one to greet him. He wasn't a hero. He kept the tags around his neck as a reminder. He kept them in plain sight in case he ever forgot his name.

An old man sat down on the bench beside him, smiled, and opened a newspaper. He looked nice enough. The young man thought about his memories. There seemed to be too many of them. They were all so stale and half forgotten. He wished he could just leave them all behind. He thought about how many memories the old man must have had. He must have lost many loved ones, maybe even himself a few times. The young man wanted nothing to do with it. He didn't want any more memories.

"I hate this place." He said to the old man.

"Hmm?" He folded the paper in his lap.

"This place. I hate it."

"Why's that?" He looked curiously at the young man.

"It's too cold. You know? It's just too damn cold."

The old man wasn't sure what to say or what to do. So, he nodded, lifted himself from the bench, and walked out of sight. It wasn't uncommon. Others have done the same. The young man had grown accustomed to people leaving without warning. Most of the people he had cared about left the same way.

He sat at the station a little longer than usual, and thought about the trains. They all had a destination. They were all bound for somewhere. For a moment, he found himself wishing he was a train, just to know the feeling of having somewhere to be. He walked across the station, bought another cup of coffee, and sat down at a different bench. The view was nicer from the new one. He could see all the people, the trains, and the tracks. He could even see the moon sitting in the sky as dusk drew in the night. It was beautiful.

He started to cry. He wasn't sure what caused it. Maybe nothing caused it, and maybe everything did. The people kept walking by him. One by one, they would look, whisper to someone near them, move on, and forget the young man was ever there. There was no consideration. There was no concern. There were just people, the trains, and the young man. Even in the crowd, he felt isolated and alone.

People hurried past him when it was announced that their train was boarding. It gave him an idea. So, he walked out onto the platform, and he kept walking until he reached the end of it. There was a fence there, but it didn't matter. The young man jumped down and followed the tracks. He could hear people yelling at him from the platform. He ignored them, and sat down on the tracks in front of the train. Then he stared blankly at everything in front of him, waited, and listened.

He heard the anger in the broken voices of the people on the platform. He also heard crickets chirping around him and chose to listen to them instead. One of them jumped onto his leg. He stared at it and smiled. He thought it would jump off, but it didn't. It sat there motionless. The young man liked it. He liked the company. He pictured himself, on a different day, sitting at a bench beside the cricket. He pictured it with a cup of coffee and maybe a cigarette. The thought amused him. He leaned back, rested his body on the tracks, and looked up at the sky. He forgot about the world. He forgot about his idea. He was comfortable.

The passengers were asked to vacate the train and wait in the station, and the police were called. They gave up on yelling. It was obvious that he wasn't going to move. Their voices faded, and the young man enjoyed the sound of the silence. The people inside were frustrated. They were all going to be a little late to wherever they were going.

(8:00 PM) The Young Woman and the Papers

She looked carefully at the notes and underlined something.

"Check this out." She said to him.

"What is it?" He put down his coffee mug.

"Most people are unhappy," she read. "But they make it a point to try and be happy." She smiled and sipped her tea. "I think that is everything."

In the evening, after the sun set over the water, and the fishermen packed up for the day, and the docks were quiet and empty, a low hum could be heard from a motor engine, and the birds perched up on the docks and on the ships.

She was reading the papers and notes she had picked up from the day. She stared out the window at the water and watched the birds scatter as a boy on an electric scooter rode by on the sidewalk. And she lit a cigarette, blew the smoke out carefully from her lips, and counted the stars. At night, tucked neatly and cleanly in bed, she would dream about the gunshot and the sirens, and she would be up for the day and collect new papers and new notes, and sit beside the window, and try again to collect the pieces of herself.

A.B. Hughes

(9:00 PM) The Man and the Rain

It was raining the real heavy sort of rain, and it was freezing. The young man watched it from outside the bar safe beneath the roof, and made special note of the way it appeared beneath the streetlamps. It was dark and the lights were all on. He stared across the street to a strip-mall, and watched the rain drip off the neon lights from some of the stores.

He should have been home an hour before, but he did not have a car, and didn't want to walk in the rain if he could avoid it. He checked his phone; four missed calls from her, all from her, and he put his phone back into his pocket. It wasn't that he was trying to avoid talking to her, but he knew it was only going to be about the divorce, and the more he thought about it, the sadder he got at the possibility of not being able to see his son again. He shook the thoughts away, and when they returned, he shook them again. And when that failed too, he turned back inside the bar and drank another beer.

There were a few young and beautiful girls in the place, locked tightly in their groups, and it was fine that they did that. He didn't want them anyway. There was an arrogance that came with a pretty girl, and if they thought they were pretty since childhood, their personalities suffered because of it. He was content enough with his beer, and the hockey game that played on the small television, and the sound of the rain as it hit the roof.

(9:30 PM) The Girl and the Music

She remembers the sound of the music that would come in through the window on those late Friday nights when they lived above the old café on Washington Street. The café attracted all sorts of men; the vagabond with a guitar, the black jazz saxophonist, the local folk singers and rock bands trying to make it big. But when the music was good, she'd open the window, dim the lights, and lean on the windowsill with a pillow and dream a few silent little dreams of being a somebody; the type of somebody who could stay late at the café, and meet all the artists as they'd come in looking for their chance at success, the type of somebody who could sing there and see people who like to hear her sing there.

But when it would get too late, and her husband would return from work, she would be unable to listen anymore. The window would be shut, there would be a short inaudible exchange of groans, the television would be turned on, and a late dinner would be started. Hardly any words would be spoken. And dinner would be served, still with fewer words. And silent little dreams would be put on hold again for the night.

9:45 PM

Over, and over, and over; like clock-work, night after night, and hour after hour. I'm tired of seeing her when I close my eyes. She isn't welcome in my head, and the longer she stays, the more I wish to drink her out; drink until it all fades away, until it's all gone dark and the feelings drown. Then I'll pour myself another drink and toast to the end of my innocence, or my pride, or my self-respect. It's all gone now, but she knows this already. It's an old story. Her eyes reflect it too, but she's too stubborn to admit it. We're both too stubborn. So, we swallow back the pain, wave our hands before a lamp to make sure that we're still there, and die a little each night.

(10:30 PM) In the Starlit Night

The man sat calmly in a chair. A cup of coffee, a package of cigarettes, and an unfinished book sat on a table beside him. He was outside on the porch, and from there with only minimal light, he could see the stars without having to strain his eyes too much, and he liked to look at them. It was chilly out that time of year.

As he stared out at the stars, he thought about how each one seemed to remind him of someone different; people from his past, people he cared little for, and people he cared deeply for, people that no longer existed but in the stars and in his memories.

A hunting gun stood unloaded against the wall of the cabin. It was an old shotgun that had been in its prime once, thought that was a long time ago. The man didn't use it anymore, but he liked to look at it and hold it every now and then.

His wife came onto the porch with a small throw-blanket in her hands. "Cover up, dear." She said. "You don't want to get sick." She put the blanket over the man's legs and torso.

"Thank you." He said. "But I'll be alright." He took a sip of coffee. The man adored his wife. She was a good

25

woman, and he had been loyal and good to her throughout the years. She was not his first wife, but she was the best, and he sometimes liked to pretend that it had only been the two of them all along.

"Do you think Charlie will visit soon?" He asked her, turning his head from the night sky.

"Oh, I don't know." She said. "He's been really busy with work and the kid"

"He's a good man. He was a good boy too, do you remember?"

"Hardly ever in trouble."

"Except for that one time, anyway." He turned to look back at the stars.

"Are you feeling alright, dear?" She walked closer to him and placed her hand on his head.

"I'm okay." He said.

"No, you're burning up."

"I'm okay. Maybe your hands are a little cold right now."

"You should come into bed." She said. "And I'll take your temperature."

"Martha, do you think Charlie knows that I love him?"

"Of course he does."

"Does he know that I think he's a good man?"

"Why are you talking like this?"

The man looked at the table beside him, then at the old shotgun, and then looked back to the sky. "I'm just not sure if I told him often enough."

"Come on now." She said. "It's time for bed."

"In a moment. I want to finish smoking and clean up out here."

She went inside to find the thermometer. On the porch, the man pulled a cigarette from the package and lit it. He then carefully stood to his feet and picked up the shotgun. He had remembered it feeling lighter once, or maybe he had just been stronger. He held it to his shoulder and imagined there was a buck out on the field, but it was heavy and he could not hold it properly. He remembered the shells were kept in a box in the shed, and he thought for a moment that he would like to fire the gun again, so he left the porch to find them.

After he left the porch, and his wife noticed he was taking longer than usual to come inside, she went outside to check on him. He wasn't there. She looked around, but she could not see him. "Thomas?" She called out. "Thomas where are you?" There was no response, just the sound of crickets and the night, and then there was the sound of the shotgun being carried from the shed to Martha's ears before vanishing off in the starlit night.

(11:00 PM) Going Home

I didn't fly back into Philly like I had wanted. They sent me to Atlantic City. I was going home. That's all any of us really want. I arrived late. I can't remember the exact time, but the sun was no longer out and it was raining. I called a cab to take me from the airport to the bus terminal.

When we're away for too long, we're always optimistic about returning home. Reality doesn't set in until we're back in our old environment, and we realize that nothing has changed. Though, I suppose, nothing ever really changes. Only our outlooks change. Mine had definitely changed, for better or worse.

It was cold in New Jersey, much colder than it had been in Georgia, and I was bald. I thought the official policy was to return us home the same way we had arrived. I'm pretty sure I had arrived with hair. I pulled my olive hat down over my ears and walked into the terminal. I bought a one-way ticket home. The bus wasn't going to board for an hour or two. I sat down and looked around at the other people. They all looked either lost or broken. I didn't want to wait around with them, so I grabbed my bag and went outside for a cigarette.

I thought about the Army again, but I didn't want to. Lord knows, I didn't want to. There were so many things I didn't get to do. I had no idea where my life was headed. There was a café up the street somewhere, and since I had time to kill, I figured I'd walk to it.

I never got that far. A hooker stopped me for a cigarette a few blocks from the terminal. She talked to me for a bit, but I can't remember the conversation. She was dull though, I remember that.

We went to a motel room. She was prepared; I wasn't. She took off her coat and dropped her dress. My mind was off the Army for the time being, but when I took off my shirt, she noticed my dog-tags.

"Are you in the Army?" She asked.

"I was."

I was glad she didn't say anything else. I wouldn't have known what to tell her. I certainly wouldn't have told her that I was discharged on account of mental instability, or that I hadn't been a soldier for nearly as long as I would have liked. I took off the rest of my clothes.

When I left the motel, I looked at my watch, realized I had missed my bus, and lit up a cigarette. The city looked awful at night and in the rain. I started to walk back to the terminal. I just wanted to go home. I wanted to lie in my bed and maybe wake up.

On my way, I noticed a homeless man across the street. He was collecting empty cans. He had a special kind of look to him; the kind of look you get when everything in your life has gone wrong and you just don't give a shit anymore. Above him was the Trump Plaza.

I didn't miss the bus a second time. I wasn't going to be home until eleven, and I had no choice left but to think. I couldn't run away any longer. Memories stormed my mind like a hurricane. I realized that going home wasn't going to solve anything. I leaned back in my chair, and stared out the window at the vanishing city lights.

(11:30 PM) The Drunk

There was a woman I met at the hotel bar in Minneapolis. There was nothing remarkable about her, but I had lost myself in a bottle of whiskey. At the time, it did not matter that she wasn't beautiful. At the time, nothing really mattered. There weren't any thoughts in my head. I was drunk and she was interested.

"So, what do you do for a living?" She asked after I bought her a drink.

"Does it matter?" I asked.

"Of course it matters." She laughed. "That's a silly question."

"Oh."

"So, what do you do?" She smiled.

"Well, I'm sort of a writer." I said.

The woman drank her martini. I had the bartender bring her another. I couldn't understand why women like her would flirt with the drunk in the bar. Maybe they thought that he was the only one who would find interest in them, and there was probably truth to that. I suppose I couldn't judge them though. They may have been the women seducing the drunk, but I was still the drunk.

"That must be exciting." She smiled. It was a fake smile.

"It isn't."

"Well, I suppose I wouldn't know." She faked another smile.

It was a lousy conversation and a waste of time. After all, we both knew where it was going to end up. There was always a weird etiquette involved with picking up women at a bar that never made any sense to me. If the desire was to have sex, couldn't we just skip past all the bullshit? The human animal has evolved just enough to reason that it is still primitive.

"Are you from around here?" She asked.

"No, Philadelphia."

"So, what brings you all the way to Minneapolis then, Mr. Writer?"

"You know, that's a good question, and there's probably an answer to it. Would you let me know if you find out?"

"You're funny." She laughed.

I had the bartender bring her a third Martini. I was growing tired of the conversation just like I had grown tired of everything else in my life. I wasn't happy. The woman had not noticed the misery though. They rarely ever do. Even if she had, she would have just moved on to another drunken man and drank more free drinks. At least, that's what they usually did.

I had a wife, but I wasn't thinking about her. I left her back in Philadelphia. I think I left my heart and my pride there as well. I wasn't sure what I was running away from or where I was headed. I just had to leave. Nothing was the same since the kid died. I knew I couldn't take the pain forever. I had gone half-way around the country, but the pain followed wherever I went. No amount of loose women or alcohol could numb the swelling in my heart. A father isn't meant to lose his son.

The woman became more upfront the more she drank. She started touching my leg under the table. I figured another martini would do the trick and had the bartender prepare it. I knew that sleeping with her wasn't going to solve any of my problems, but I was at least going to try.

"So, your room or mine?" She asked.

I don't know how I answered, but we made it back to my hotel room. I almost forgot the reason she came back with me, and I was about to pour us more drinks when I noticed she was undressing. Just like everything else about her, her body wasn't remarkable. It was just kind of a body. I imagined it would be warm if nothing else.

"Are you coming?" She called out from the bed.

"Just a minute." I said as I swallowed a drink.

"Well, hurry."

So, I hurried. I knew she wasn't going to like it, but it wasn't about her. I didn't care about her, and I wasn't going to pretend that I cared just for her benefit. She'd get satisfaction out of that. I wasn't prepared to give it to her. She'd have to find some other poor sap for that. There were plenty of them down at the bars.

I couldn't get the kid out of my head though. No matter what I did, or how much I drank, I'd see his face everywhere. I'd close my eyes and see him in the casket. I'd see his mother's tear-stained eyes in every woman I slept with. I didn't know how to escape it. I started to tear up.

"What's wrong?" She asked.

I didn't reply to her. I knew she wouldn't be able to understand, and I didn't want her to understand. I climbed off her and sat at the corner of the bed. I ran my fingers through my hair and tried to wipe the tears away.

"I'm going to leave now." She said.

"Just fucking leave then." I shouted and she scrambled to put her clothes on.

When she was gone, I put on my underwear, grabbed a bottle of whiskey, and sat by the window. I felt alone again. Everyone who ever loved me was in my past. I drank some of the bottle, and leaned my head against the glass and looked out at my memories reflected in the night blanketed sky.

(12:15 AM) The Old Woman and the Rain

The wind shook the walls, and rattled the windows. It was a quarter past midnight. All the lights from the apartment building across the street had been turned off. Only the neon glow from the liquor store down the block remained, illuminating bits of the broken night in waves of subtle red. The rain came down in solid, steady streams, shining under the streetlamps and the neon.

The old woman sat on her balcony beneath the shelter of her neighbor's above. She had a glass of moscato beside her on the table, a package of Winston Light that she held onto; afraid they might blow away if she were to set them down. She wore a big white coat, and the collar had been turned into her neck. She was listening to the sound of the rain.

It reminded her of someone from long ago, from a time before she was married, before war broke out in Europe, before there were all those things separating them. He always loved to listen to the rain.

It was never appropriate for a lady to sit out like that, but since she was old, and her husband passed, all her children moved away, she didn't care about what was appropriate anymore, and she'd sit out if she wanted to.

The city from her balcony gleamed, and if she were to squint, it would appear to her no different than a water-color painting. It was an art gallery all her own, and she felt perfect there in the beauty of it, and she wondered if there was another tired old soul out there in that wild city, transfixed in it just the way she was. And she thought, 'what lonely lives we all must live together'. She laughed a sweet laugh quietly to herself, and she smiled a smile that could have been no more beautiful if she were young.

And soon, she would turn in for bed, but she would leave the window open, and she would fall asleep to the sound of the rain just like they used to do all those years ago. And she would be reunited with him in her dreams. And she would fall in love with him all over again in her dreams.

12:45 AM

What happened to the time? Has it faded away like everything else? And what about sleep? Did I ever sleep? I can't remember. I don't know how I got here. I'm not sure where here is. Am I lost? I feel like I'm lost. God, help me. I think I might be lost.

(1:00 AM) In Search of Something Warm

"Are you tired?" She asked.

"No, not really." I said. "I'm just thinking.

"About what?" She turned over in the sheets to face me.

"I'm not really sure."

There was a candle lit by the window. It wasn't enough; it was too cold. The wind picked up, and the rain danced across the window. There was a bad storm. The weatherman said it was one of the worst in years. But, it was just cold outside, and the candle wasn't enough. She moved in closer to me. She couldn't have known that I didn't love her. I had tried to, but it wasn't enough.

"Is everything okay?" She asked

"Yeah, why shouldn't it be?"

"You're so quiet." She whispered.

The candle flickered, and the wind rattled the walls. I didn't want to talk to her, but somehow, within the silence and the quest for warmth, I always did anyway. It's all so sad and stale; it's always so stale. And after all, what can really be done about it? There was just the echo of a lost little dream bouncing around out there in the rain. I leaned my head against the

41

pillow and stared into her eyes, hoping to find something within them.

"Why should we have to speak?"

"I just thought—"

The wind came again, and she turned to look at it. I thought about all the others who had been in her spot before. There was one who came to mind the most. The last time I saw her, she was boarding a train to some far off coast in search of a dream. She was certainly beautiful; all the best ones are. I wondered if she ever found what she was looking for. There were others, but they were far less interesting. I thought about each of them, the ones I could remember, for a moment. I didn't really think much about the one beside me.

She was a good woman, from what I could tell, and I was just lost. It was only a few days before that I had stumbled half-dazed through the sick and pale city streets. My blood-shot eyes searched for answers out there, but I only found the drunken mess that had become of my life. I wasn't the man for her, and I doubt that I was the one for any of them. The candle dimmed again.

"I wonder when the storm will pass." She said.

"By morning at the latest."

"I have work in the morning."

I never tried to lead on that I loved her. I never lied to her. I had tried to keep it safe and easy. Perhaps I had hoped once that there could be a flame, I was tired of the cold, but a good flame required fuel, and I had very little left to give.

"I'm gonna have a cigarette." I said.

She did not reply. She turned her head over into the pillow.

I put on pants, grabbed my cigarettes from atop the dresser, and slid over to the balcony. I could see the extent of the storm from there; the rain fell like needles. Across the street, I could see the neon-lights of a bar pierce through the darkness; the rain glistened from them and dripped like blood. I lit my cigarette. My neighbor was playing Mozart on the piano. I always hated Mozart, but I listened quietly to it anyway.

When he finished playing, I put out my cigarette and went back to the room. She was sound asleep when I got to the bed. I pulled the blanket up to her shoulders. I had liked to look at her body before, but I couldn't see the point in it anymore. I sat down, pulled a bottle of whiskey out from its hiding spot, and blew out the candle.

A.B. Hughes

(1:30 AM) A Veteran at the Park

The veteran sat and stared at the rain bouncing off the cars in the parking lot. He watched the way the water came in under the lights. It was an empty night, and the young man, with no more cares in the world, sat motionless on the park bench. His mind wandered between times and places, and he wanted very much not to think of the things that troubled him. He thought of meaningless gestures; a wave from a passing stranger walking his dog down the sidewalk, a child's glance, a squirrel doing nothing at all; an anxiety attack for no real reason. And the young man thought of a girl he remembered from a film. He imagined her walking down the sidewalk, maybe sitting beside him on the bench. And he imagined that he would do nothing; perhaps only nod, and then admire the silence. But he probably wouldn't even do that. The young man closed his eyes, squeezed them tightly, but he could still see the nightmares peer back in at him. He could feel nothing but his own beating heart. He was grateful that it was still beating. He could not say the same for some of the other people he once knew. He just wanted the nightmares to go away.

1:45 AM

We could feel the pull of our lives dragging us unsatisfyingly here and there. We did not know our worth as people, and perhaps that was our fault. We allowed them all to break us down so completely until all that was left was a skeleton that still had nightmares.

(2:00 AM) Late Night Wine

There is wine on the desk. The man sips at the bottle every now and then, and he hates that he does it. He is unhappy. He tastes loneliness. He can't drink the ghosts away. He can't make himself whole again. He wonders if he was ever whole. And it goes on and on this way until the bottle runs dry, as it must do every night. Then he sits for a while, stares at the blue-glowing alarm clock, and wonders, worries; always wondering and worrying.

It is raining outside. It's the kind of rain that would be nice in the summer, but it is not the summer. The water heater is busted. There aren't enough groceries in the fridge. The shirts are all wrinkled.

Sometimes, real late at night, he can almost still hear her voice crack through into this world. He knows she is gone, but he can hear her voice, and that makes him miss her more. He would like to be with her tonight, to hold her, smell her hair. She was always warm and bright. She could make eyes light up just by being in a place. He was never like that. He is quiet, and people only ever like him when he is drunk.

The problem with being alone at night is that one is left with only the most honest form of himself. It is different during the day; there are reasons to be strong. Anyone can be strong

47

during the day. It is the test of a first rate character to also be strong at night, when there is no one.

So, the man stares at the clock ticking his life away, and he hears her voice, and he knows that she is not really there, but he hears it completely, and she says, "You walk around life like you're angry at something."

"I am angry." He whispers.

"What are you angry about?"

"I haven't decided yet." He says, but it is a lie, and he knows that it is a lie. He is angry that she took a piece of his life with her, and the only thing he has now is wine and the blue light from a clock that won't stop ticking.

(2:30 AM) For that Moment

The wind was beating against the walls, and the rain splashed across the windows. A man and a woman were lying together on the bed. The woman was asleep. Her body was wrapped around the man, and her head rested on his chest. She was warm with him. She never slept so easily than she did when she was with him.

The man was awake. He could not take his eyes off her. The lights from the passing cars reflected off the rain and danced across her face. It was a beautiful face. He never wanted to stop looking at her, but he knew that one day he would have to. He understood well that nothing lasts forever. Regardless of how long he would like to hold her, he would eventually have to let go.

The man kissed her cheek and held her a little tighter. He wished that time would stop moving for just that moment. He wished that the night would never have to end. He did not want to see it go. He did not want the rain and the wind to ever stop. Above all, he did not want to see the sun come up. He knew it would never be that perfect again.

He was terrified of the unknown future. He was terrified of having to face change. Life had always demanded so much of him. Rarely did he have perfect moments. He kissed her again and moved her hair away from her face.

The woman was not afraid of change. She embraced it as a fact of life. After all, one should not fear what is unknown. She dreamed of happy things. She always had pleasant dreams when she was with him. For her, the moment was everlasting, because she would carry it with her the rest of her life.

He touched her lips. He was careful not to wake her. They were lovely lips. The longer he looked at her, the more he realized that he was in love with her. The feeling crept up on him, and it was a terrifying one. The only thing he could think about was how much it was going to hurt when he would lose her.

Once again, he wished that time would stop for them, but it cannot do that. "I think I love you." He whispered. She did not wake up. He knew that in the morning, he would not say it. He was not ready to say it, and he was not sure if he would ever be. He felt it, and that was all that mattered to him. He kissed her one last time and quietly fell asleep.

2:45 AM

You climb out of the hole just to realize you're all alone again. Those who claim to love you are nowhere to be seen. Mother, can't you see I'm better than this? Please, don't abandon me. Please. I can't stand being left to crawl on my own. They all leave me; all of them. Father, you left me too. I was too young to cry out for you to stay. You left me in the cradle. Please, World, do not leave me in the void. Please, Life, do not leave me without breath. Please, Time, do not leave me kicking the tin cans of my memories. Please, don't go.

(3:00 AM) At a Rest Stop on the Freeway

"Nights like these don't come around too often anymore." He whispered to her in the bed.

"What do you mean?" She smiled.

"Well, you know." He paused briefly, locating the right words from some hidden spot in his mind. "I love you, and it is a very nice night."

The man sat alone in the rest stop cafeteria, somewhere near the wall between the Quizno's and the Starbucks, sipped at his overpriced coffee, and thought about why he was leaving. There was nothing left, nothing back there, nothing left. And outside the window, he watched as a big eighteen-wheeler was being filled with gasoline. The driver got out and said something to the attendant, smiled, and slapped him on the back. And the man in the cafeteria thought of where the truck would be headed, St. Paul, Indianapolis, Seattle, Tucson? The destination did not matter. It would all be better, he thought. Any place would be better.

So, the man sat a little longer; unsure of where to go, unsure of everything else. He pulled out an oversized map, and a circle had been drawn around Baltimore. It was his home, and he did not want to turn around.

"There's certainness to it." He said and brushed her hair aside.

She blushed and moved in, rested her head on his chest trying to be as close as possible. "Haven't you learned that nothing is ever certain?"

He smiled.

"Certainty takes the beauty out of things." She looked him in the eyes. "Don't you think?"

The man drew a line to Pittsburgh. That's it, he thought, that's where I'll go. It must be nice this time of year. But the man remained seated still for a while. He watched the people come and go from the rest stop. He stayed seated there for so long that he watched most of the restaurants close one by one, and if not for the truckers who came and went outside, he'd have felt confident in knowing he was all alone in the world.

He wanted to tell her that there were some things they could know for certain, but he knew that she was right. "This is a very nice night, because I am here with you now." He said.

"I love you." She reassured him.

At last, he left the rest stop, fumbled in the car with his keys, and pulled out a photograph of her. She was remarkable and beautiful, and he missed her very much. He fought back tears, started the car, and pulled out on the road to Pittsburgh or some other place; some place to dull the ache, some place to be a something and not more of the great nothing that had filled inside of him.

He wanted not to think about it, but like most things, the thoughts came anyway. He remembered it being a Sunday when he got the call that she was in the hospital. The man was drunk, drove right through the red light. He didn't stop for a mile after. He didn't even know what happened. He tore right through her, and she did not make it long. But she fought the strongest fight that she could. Pittsburgh will be nice, he thought as he wiped his face with his sleeve. Yeah, Pittsburgh will be nice.

"I would very much like to be here with you forever." He said to her.

"And I would very much like to be here with you forever too." She said and they kissed.

(3:30 AM) Remembering Vera

Something was wrong. He was too distant. His eyes once hung on her every movement, but they wandered between everything then like he was searching for something. She missed him more than anything, but she could not find that blue-eyed man of hers, though he lay in plain sight beside her. How many cold nights did he lie awake warming her? She remembered it all vividly. He was a good man, and a good man is hard to come by; she knew that well.

She hardly thought of herself as a good woman, but it wasn't the time to be insecure. It was too cold in that bed, in that night and time, and she had to believe she was good; she had to be strong and confident in herself. It was too early in the year for doubt anyway. It's meant for summer, she thought, and early fall too, but not now; not now with all this rain. And as she thought, she heard him breathe beside her; deep and calm, in and out, all at once like a wave. And she wished no greater wish than to drift along with him, in warmer waters, forever.

He reached out to touch her, to wrap his arm around her, but he was asleep, and she could not trust it. His cold fingers made the hair on her arm uneasy, and they stood to attention. He's a ghost, she thought, or a skeleton stretching his bones from beyond the grave; nothing more than this, nothing ever more than this.

She wanted to cry, but she knew it was too cold for it. She brushed away his arm, mummified herself in the blanket the best she could, closed her eyes, and began to imagine. Flowers, she thought, I need flowers; why is there never anything pretty? And what else is there in this barren no-man's land to make this lifeless, loveless night any better? Give me clouds and dew drops; no more of this acid rain and fallout. Give me a warm mid-August evening; there I can breathe and live again, there I can be free. But as hard as she tried, she could not imagine warmth as great as what she used to feel with him.

She knew she was bound to cry, and she wanted to cry, and scream out against the horror of it all. Flowers, she reminded herself, where might I get them? I need them, no I need him, but they're pretty; not many things are pretty anymore, not the moon, not his eyes, not the rain, not anything at all. And she hated herself for thinking that way, but she could not help it. Nothing could ever be the same again.

She refused to turn around and look at him. He's just a phantom, she thought, just a corpse in the bed. He was good and warm once. And she thought of the days and nights that he hung to her and her to him, and she could not stay in that bed any longer. She quietly shifted herself from it, and tip-toed to the fire escape. She kept the blanket wrapped around her like a shawl for warmth, opened the window, and stared out at Manhattan. It was perfect when they moved there, before he left her alone, and she missed the time they had spent together. Her eyes dampened, and she climbed out the window.

There was a flower pot out there, but there weren't any flowers; just a pool of water left by the rain. She hated it. And in that moment, the only thing she wanted to do was jump, to end the damned thing that had become of her life, to lose the memories of him, of the warmth, of those mid-August evenings, and of those pretty flowers. She didn't want any of it any longer. She looked over the rail at the wet ground below and watched the way the rain bounced off the pavement. There was so much sadness, so much anger, and all she knew to do was cry, so she cried, and she screamed, and she threw the flower pot from the fire-escape. The loud sound of it woke him from his sleep, but he couldn't do anything about it, so he just listened.

She sat down in the corner where the wall of the building joined with the rail, and stared up to the sky as the water washed over her face and her tears. And she remembered a song, and she tried to sing "Does anybody here remember—" But she froze up and she couldn't sing it. "Oh, Vera, you were wrong." She said. "You were so wrong." And he heard her still from where he was in the bedroom.

Then she couldn't help but think about it all. She couldn't help but remember back when he was warm, and he said to her, "Don't cry. Everything will be okay. I'll only be gone for six months. I'll be back before you know it, and everything will be okay." And the next time she saw him, after the IED tore through his legs and his soft-tissue, he was a corpse without the jewels that were once his eyes. She missed him more than anything, and she wanted that warmth, and to drift along with him in the waves of his breath forever, but it could never be the same again. He knew her pain, but the only thing he could do was cry and whisper "I love you."

3:45 AM

Never lose yourself in any situation; maintain yourself, love yourself, grow from the strong places and learn from the weak ones until they too become strengths to get you up the mountain.

(4:15 AM) Probably Just another Moment

It was a quarter-past-four in the morning when the man checked his watch. He sat alone at the diner at a booth beside a window. He liked to sit and look out the window, even though there wasn't anything worth looking at. There were hardly any cars on the road, and the only light he could see came from the neon glow of the liquor store across the street. He stared at it for a bit and wondered how much he'd need to drink to forget everything. The man was troubled, but he didn't like to admit it. He needed help, but he'd never ask for it. He was convinced that he could solve his problems on his own, but the older he got, the more he began to realize that he couldn't. Too much time had passed before him, and he wasn't able to keep up with the ticking clock. He was lost.

He thought about his time in the service; thought about the guns, and the pain, and the brothers lost. He thought about those who slipped away, the ones he forced away, and the forgotten children that vanished in plain sight. He thought about how he didn't want to think anymore. For a brief second, he felt sure that he might cry, but the tears did not come. When the first light of dawn could be seen from the window, and the morning people came in for coffee and a smile, the man was no longer in the diner.

63

5:00 AM

The soldier lay awake just before dawn and counted the ceiling tiles above his bed. "Too much." He whispered, and he had seen too much. All the men had seen too much. But it was not the war that had disturbed them all so greatly, it was the guilt of feeling responsible for it, and for their mothers, wives, children, it was the guilt of feeling responsible for all of it. He'll never be the same, and it was obvious to him as he lay there, staring at the busted-up ceiling tiles. He didn't want to dream anymore, he only wanted to be left alone, to stay there and stare up at the ceiling forever; to forget about everything forever.

(5:30 AM) Cigarettes and the Rain

A few miles south of my home there is a park that, over the years, has become a part of me. It lies along the banks of a winding river as it becomes a bay, just before it joins hands with the Atlantic. My greatest thoughts have all formed around that body of water. I witnessed both the birth and the death of dreams drift along with the current. I've felt my heart beat beneath its surface.

In my times of strength and weakness, I would tie the laces of my warned down combat boots, brave whatever weather was granted me, and walk the half hour to the park. That night wasn't any different. There wasn't anything unique about it. All nights can be both horrible and pleasant. The only difference between the two is how we choose to look at it. That night was neither. It was just another night.

It rained for a while. I watched it pour down from my bedroom window. I remember wondering about all of the lost souls; all the lost and weary men and women out in the rain. There must have been so many of them trapped by the walls of their own lives. We're all trapped in some way. I thought about the few who tried to run. Who really knew what they were running from; the rain, the night, the darkness in their mind? Who can ever know?

The rain stopped and left a fog. It was beautiful. There's beauty to be found in everything. I stepped out into the fog. The rain left the air stale and humid. Thoughts were racing through my mind, like a freight train, leading me through the darkness.

I've seen things crawl out from the shadows that I still can't understand. In my mind, in my dreams, silhouettes and apparitions of long since forgotten hours come back to haunt me. They remind me of the times when I was too weak to save myself.

As I walked through the fog, I thought about how the hours never stopped, not even for a moment, but they still couldn't tick fast enough. That's the problem with time; a night can be endless or pass by in a blink.

I stopped at a store along the way for a pack of cigarettes and a cup of coffee. I lit a cigarette and walked to the end of the park, the furthest I could be, and stared out at the water.

It was remarkable. In the thickness of the fog, at that hour of night, there was no distinction between the sky and the water. It was all just one, like standing in the middle of a cloud. Across the bay, a green light was flickering. I remembered that light. It had fascinated me for years. It was different then. It reflected off the mist and the water. It lit the whole sky. I was never more at peace.

I stayed there for hours. I stayed until the fog cleared and the tip of the sun could be seen on the horizon. I stayed until I could no longer see the green light. It was a powerful light. It was the light of hope. It broke through the darkness. It silenced the thoughts in my head. It was as if it whispered to me, from across the bay, the type of reassurance I needed. As if it said, "Be calm. Everything will be okay."

With morning breaking over me, I turned to walk back home. Perhaps there is nothing special about night or day. Perhaps there is nothing special about life, and it is truly just a simple thing. If mankind were only so simple, we wouldn't need a green light to remind us that everything is okay.

www.ingramcontent.com/pod-product-compliance
Lightning Source LLC
Chambersburg PA
CBHW020316150626
46552CB00022B/2906